The Hungry Toilet

AND OTHER TALES

Written and Illustrated by Jason Hall

First published in 2012

ISBN-13:
978-1481238403

The Hungry Toilet

In Cresington Park, on Cresington Lane,
There's an old public toilet with an old broken chain,
This toilet has been there for many a year,
It's revolting and putrid, most people steer clear,
So uninviting, but if you are pushed,
Choose either this toilet or go in a bush.

This old public toilet believe it or not,
Has never been closed, despite damp, despite rot,
The local town's people commissioned, complained,
But somehow or another the toilet remained.

A mystery surrounded old Cresington Town,
Over the months its numbers went down,
Locals went out for a walk in the park,
To get some fresh air, let the dog run and bark,
These very same people never came home,
Only dogs at the door, cold and alone.

Cresington Council run Cresington Park,
They are responsible for this toilet most dark,
The council employed Mrs Pungent McShark,
To clean and lock up said toilet in park.

Mrs Pungent McShark was a horrible soul,
Her face resembled a squashed sausage roll,
She was bitter and twisted, heartless and cruel,
With breath that smelt worse than a septic cesspool.

MRS PUNGENT MCSHARK

The story goes that Mrs McShark,
Had once been in love with Mr Narcbark,
He was employed as the Cresington Park Keeper,
The locals called him the Cresington Grim Reaper.

He was wicked, twisted, nasty and grey,
An encounter with Narcbark darkened your day,
His was skinny, wrinkly, bony and sour,
Stand within a foot of him, you wanted a shower.

But Narcbark finally paid the price,
The cost for living nasty not nice,
Clearing up leaves he stepped on his rake,
The handle shot up, he felt his nose break,
Knocked out cold, he fell to the deck,
Falling awkward, breaking his neck.

Lying there in a bed of leaves,
He screamed and he shouted, "Help, help me please!"
But the Cresington people ignored his cries,
Looking away, diverting their eyes,
Left there for days, he died in those leaves,
Many years on, Pungent McShark still grieves.

On the day of the funeral she swore revenge,
"They left him to die, his life I'll avenge,
I'll get them back one by one,
Narcbark my lost love, consider it done!"

Over the days she hatched her plan,
"I'll wreak revenge man by man,
Come to the park and use my loo,
That'll be the last they'll see of you."

Pungent McShark built a suction machine,
Connected up to her old park latrine,

Once you have finished you pulled on the chain,
Sucked down the bowl then into the drain.

Pungent's first victim was a lady called Kate,
Bursting to go, she just couldn't wait,
Finished, she pulled down on the chain,
Starting the suction machine up like a plane,

Into the bowl, sucked head first,
But Kate was still to experience the worst,
Flying through drains under the town,
Skidding, twirling and twisting around,
Travelling at speed through miles of pipes,
Covered in grime and used baby wipes,
At last she was exited far out to sea,
Alive, in one piece, but with no memory.

A month or so later was a Mr Joe Dench,
Running to the toilet with buttocks clenched,
Finished, he pulled down on the chain,
Starting the suction machine up again,
Into the bowl, sucked head first,
Within a split second he was fully submersed,
Skidding, twirling and twisting around,
Flying through drains under the town,
At last he was exited far out to sea,
Again, in one piece, but with no memory.

The hungry toilet did not stop there,
Swallowing Dan French and Miss Delaware,
It sucked up Miss Josephine and Phil McLight,
And poor Mr Jones late one Saturday night,
Every person swallowed was spat out to sea,
Yes, you have guessed it, with no memory.

The gossip and stories were running rife,
Were they abducted by an alien life?
Was it a tornado? Some said a black hole,
The Police were clueless, situation out of control.

People were selling and moving away,
The future of the town was gloomy and grey,
But it all came to a head one wet winter's day,
When the toilet was flushed by a poor boy named Ray.

Ray really was the very largest of boys,
His parents showered him in chocolate and toys,
He ate, and he ate, and he ate, and he ate,
And on this fateful Friday his stomach so ached.

He sat in the park, sad and alone,
Deep in his thoughts before he went home,
When all of a sudden his stomach made rumbles,
The adverse effect of eleven rhubarb crumbles,

All of a sudden he needed the lavatory,
Now in a panic, I can't repeat his vocabulary.

Running as fast as his legs would comply,
Whilst unfastening his belt buckle and fly,
Just in time he sat down on the seat,
Wishing he hadn't had so much to eat.

Finally done, he pulled down on the chain,
Starting the suction machine up once again,
The toilet was now to meet its match,
Ray was too big for the flush to dispatch.

Sucked up by his bottom cheeks first,
But now the toilet experienced the worst,
The suction machine grinded and churned,
The vacuum belts ripped as they turned.

Frozen now in a state of shock,
His huge bottom cheeks creating a block,
The grinding noises screeching out loud,
Then an explosion, and a great mushroom cloud.

The walls of the building now blown away,
The only thing left was a toilet, sat on by Ray,
The explosion drew people from near and afar,
They stood and they stared, mouths ajar.

Ray stood up and pulled up his jeans,
It really was the most extraordinary of scenes,
He spoke in a faint and slurry mumble,
"Never again will I eat rhubarb crumble."

Over the days the facts became clear,
In front of the Judge, McShark to appear,
The police discovered the suction machine,
Cresington Town now a famous crime scene.

Pungent McShark confessed to the crime,
Going to jail for a very long time,
But where were Kate and Mr Joe Dench,
Miss Delaware and Mr Dan French,
Miss Josephine and Phil McLight,
Last Mr Jones, are they alive and alright?

You'll be pleased to know they were found out to sea,
And one by one they regained memory,
Picked up by boats, one caught in a net,
Frozen and lost and of course very wet.

Over the weeks they found their way home,
Except Mr Jones who resettled in Rome,
Each one returned to a huge celebration,
Broadcast around the world on every TV station.

The forgotten hero is of course poor old Ray,
Who caused the toilet to blow up on that day,
They say every cloud has a silvery lining,
And in Ray's case it was that he quit over dining,
Ray is no longer the size of two boys,
And his parents have learnt not to shower him in toys.

THE END

LET'S TALK ABOUT THIS STORY

1. Why did the dogs turn up at the door cold and alone?

2. What was the name of the lady employed to look after the toilet?

3. What was the name of the Park Keeper?

4. Can you name any of the people swallowed by the toilet?

5. How many rhubarb crumbles did Ray eat on the fateful day?

6. Where did Mr Jones decide to resettle?

7. Do you think Ray is the hero of the story and why?

CAN YOU SPOT 10 DIFFERENCES BETWEEN THESE 2 PICTURES?

CAN YOU COMPLETE THESE RHYMING COUPLETS FROM THE HUNGRY TOILET?

1. Ray really was the very largest of boys,
His parents showered him in chocolate and ?

2. He spoke in a faint and slurry mumble,
"Never again will I eat rhubarb ?"

3. He was skinny, wrinkly, bony and sour,
Stand within a foot of him, you wanted a ?

4. Mrs Pungent McShark was a horrible soul,
Her face resembled a squashed sausage ?

5. Travelling at speed through miles of pipes,
Covered in grime and used baby ?

6. Frozen now in a state of shock,
His huge bottom cheeks creating a ?

THE HUNGRY DUMP'S REVENGE

I know a story to fill you with fear,
About a sad school built somewhere near here,
The school was rushed and built in a hurry,
And on it was spent next to no money.

It was built on top of an old rubbish tip,
Which gurgled and wurgled and sometimes would spit,
The stench was enough to make you feel sick,
While hovering above were nits licking their lips.

Into it were thrown unmentionable things,
Like old smelly nappies and hospital bins,
An old wrinkly skin and a half eaten fin,
But worst an old sewer shipped in from Berlin.

All these ingredients reacted and stirred,
They hummed and they murmured
and sometimes they purred,
Over the years they'd fermented and stewed,
A terrible concoction had unknowingly brewed.

Mr Chisel the builder who built the new school,
Had cut every corner and ignored all the rules,
He'd filled it with sand and a few broken bricks,
This pesky old builder was up to old tricks.

The foundations for certain were not built to hold,
A week since grand opening now smothered in mould,
Mr Strictly the Head phoned the builder in rage,
Mr Chisel the builder was always engaged.

The mould kept on spreading and started to stink,
Turn on the tap and sludge came up the sink,
Cracks were appearing in ceilings and floors,
The handles were falling off most of the doors.

It was morning assembly, last in were year five,
When all of a sudden the walls came alive,
They moaned and they slivered, they oozed and they creaked,
The mould was alive and starting to reek.

"Escape!" said the Head. "That Chisel's a vandal!"
But how do you open a door with no handle?
Just when they thought things couldn't get worse,
The mould began groaning its terrible curse…

"I was the tip in the town, only good for one thing,
You didn't love me I was just a big bin,
No one thought or cared what they threw into me,
You never reused and were never thrifty,
You always bought new, and threw out your old,
You ignored all the warnings and wouldn't be told,
You never repaired, you always replaced,
It's someone else's problem, that problem of waste,
Well today is the day that the rubbish gets back,
What I desire is a huge human snack,
I want boys, I want girls, I want Heads, I want teachers,
I'm bored of your rubbish, I want living creatures."

The hall started moving and started to shake,
It felt like the tremors of a minor earthquake,
Through the middle of the hall a crevice appeared,
Mr Weir was not quick enough, Mr Weir disappeared.

The crevice now split the hall completely in half,
On one side were students, on the other were staff,
Everyone stood silent awaiting their fate......
For the answer, they didn't have too long to wait.

Out came a wretched rumble and burp,
Followed by the sloppiest most slimiest slurp,
The dump sighed a moan and spat out Weir's sandal,
The Head shouted out, "It's leather it can't handle!"

"Everyone quick throw in your shoes,
Rubber and leather it simply can't chew!"
Trainers, high heels and school shoes flew in,
Shoes were the last hope of stopping the bin.

A terrible chewing and moaning was heard,
A stomachey sound so very absurd,
The most twisted, awful and horrible sound,
Like nails down blackboards or metal along ground.

School shoes and high heels had upset the dump,
It was clearly in pain and a right royal hump,
It screamed out loud, "I have indigestion,
Someone please help me, please make a suggestion."

Just at that moment, the hall doors swung open,
It was Chisel the builder, belly big as the ocean,
"So what's going on 'ere, what's the commotion?
Strictly's complaining has got me demotion."

Mr Chisel

The Head crept around and rose behind Chisel,
Whilst Chisel was picking his teeth for old grizzle,
With an almighty shove the Head pushed Chisel in,
A minute or two later came a sigh from the bin.

"For so many years I've had indigestion,
All of your rubbish is no good for digestion,
But now at last my heartburn is placid,
That big bellied Chisel's a fantastic antacid,
I can't thank you enough, I am angry no more,"
He spat Mr Weir out alive on the floor.

Feeling lucky to be here, like they'd just won the lotto,
The Governors and Head rewrote the school's motto:

We will never use builders that look too shifty,
We will always reuse and always be thrifty,
We will rarely buy new and throw out our old,
We will heed all the warnings and always be told,
We will try to repair instead of replace,
It's everyone's problem, our problem of waste.

THE END

LET'S TALK ABOUT THIS STORY

1. Can you name some of the items of rubbish thrown into the tip?

2. What was the name of the builder?

3. Which year was last into assembly?

4. What did the tip want to eat instead of rubbish?

5. What was the name of the teacher who was swallowed?

6. What did the staff and students throw in to stop the tip?

7. What do you think is the message in this story?

CAN YOU SPOT 7 DIFFERENCES BETWEEN THESE 2 PICTURES?

CAN YOU COMPLETE THESE RHYMING COUPLETS FROM THE HUNGRY DUMP'S REVENGE?

1. Out came a wretched rumble and burp,
Followed by the sloppiest most slimiest ?

2. Into it were thrown unmentionable things,
Like old smelly nappies and hospital ?

3. "I can't thank you enough, I am angry no more,"
He spat Mr Weir out alive on the ?

4. He'd filled it with sand and a few broken bricks,
This pesky old builder was up to old ?

5. Through the middle of the hall a crevice appeared,
Mr Weir was not quick enough, Mr Weir ?

6. We will try to repair instead of replace,
It's everyone's problem, our problem of ?

COPS AND SLOBBERS

Roderick Robinson the robber,
Was always in and out of bother,
From the corner of his mouth,
There was always dripping slobber.

He'd creep in through your window,
To get in to your house,
He was a true professional,
As quiet as a mouse.

He'd steal anything and everything,
And everything and anything,
He'd steal your dad's old slippers,
Yes, the ones that smell of kippers,
And your toaster and your telly,
And if she's asleep, your Auntie Nelly.

He'd steal the pyjamas you are sleeping in,
And you wouldn't even stir,
And if you had a cat he would even steal its fur,
It really makes no difference to him what he takes or took,
He's a skinny, sneaky, slimy, grimy, naughty little crook.

But as I told you from the start,
He was always in and out of bother,
'Cos from the corners of his mouth,
There was always dripping slobber.

When Inspector Spouse inspected the house,
For clues to solve the crime,
It didn't take him long,
To step and slip in slobber slime,
"That slobbering Roderick Robinson!"

Inspector Spouse would curse,
And when there was no one else about,
I'm sure he said much worse,
"When will he learn that slobbering and
robbering don't mix?"
But as they say, you cannot teach,
A dog to change,
And learn new tricks.

Poor old Roderick Robinson tried many different jobs,
For example in a cafe owned and run by Rascal Rob,
The customers would ask for salt and vinegar on their chips,
And maybe some tomato sauce on the side in which to dip,
But no one asked for Roderick's slobber in their food,
It really was enough to make you ill, and spoil your mood.

Next he was a window cleaner with his bucket and his cloth,
But his ladder got all slippery from dripping slobber froth,
He slipped and fell and broke his legs,
Both his arms and cracked his head,
He spent a month in pain and plaster, lying in his bed.

Let's get back to our story now we know
more about double R,
Perhaps you're feeling sorry for him
can I hear you whisper, Ahhhhh?

The hopeless Roderick Robinson
planned one last big, big job,
It was going to be world famous,
The go down in history kind of rob.

The poor old Queen of England,
At Buckingham Palace in London town,
Was to be Roderick's target,
He was going to steal her crown.

He dug an enormous tunnel,
For miles and miles underground,
It finished under the palace,
And it started from his lounge.

If his calculations were accurate,
He should be underneath the palace,
Time to put his costume on,
Disguise - a chambermaid called Alice.

He pushed up a single floorboard,
And slowly peeped around,
Quietly as he does it, dare not make a sound.

He slipped into the hallway,
Then darted from room to room,
Like a mouse chased by a cat,
Closely followed by a broom,
He filled his bag up as he went and never missed a thing,
Silver plates and paperweights and even a napkin ring.

Then he saw it sitting there shimmering under the lights,
Polished, shining, immaculate, such an awe inspiring sight,
He looked around and then around,
Then looked around once more,
Laser beams were surrounding the crown,
He counted twenty four.

He bent, split and twisted, tearing his pants at the seams,
Manoeuvring himself in and out of alarmed laser beams,
Finally in the middle he picked up the priceless crown,
Carefully putting it in his bag,
Wrapped in the Queen's dressing gown.

Returning through the beams was the final thing to do,
So very, very nearly there,
Could he see this thing through?

Roderick now had a single laser beam to go,
When a glob of slobber slob began to drip and show,
There it was, hanging there,
Swinging to and fro,
But then the glob lost its grip,
The rest is in slow mo.

He watched his dreams disappear of being a millionaire,
As he saw the glob slowly glide down through the air,
Eventually the glob struck the laser beam,
And within a millisecond the alarms began to scream,
Roderick Robinson was frozen there,
Dressed as a chambermaid,
Feeling rather stupid, feeling rather afraid.

Then he heard a voice, a voice he'd heard before,
"Good evening Double R, it's the long arm of the law!

I visited you at home Double R, to find that you were out,
You left your back door open so I took a nose about,
That tunnel in your lounge led me to this place,
Your slippy, slimy, slobber trail wasn't hard to trace,"
It was of course Inspector Spouse,
Standing, stationed, in the Queen's house.

Then slobbering Roderick Robinson,
Began to weep and sob,
"It was meant to be world famous,
The go down in history kind of rob,
But once again I've messed it up,
Foiled and cheated by dribbling slob!"

Then they heard a voice,
A voice they'd both heard before,
"Good evening ladies and gentlemen,
Tell me, what's all this fuss, what's all the furore?
And please do you mind Madam, not dribbling on my floor!"

It was Her Royal Highness, Her Majesty the Queen,
Wearing just her night gown,
Looking cold, and looking mean.

"Good evening M'lady, please allow me to explain,
Inspector Spouse at your service,
Scotland Yard, the very same,
This is the notorious burglar known as Double R,
A criminal with a record that stretches wide and far,
There in his arms he steals M'lady's crown,
Wrapped in M'lady's very own dressing gown."

"Well, what do you have to say for yourself,
You so called Double R?
I've been looking for that dressing gown,
My butler's even looking in the car,
I'm absolutely frozen and now you steal my crown,
It looks like your slobbering has really let you down."

"Your Majesty, your Majesty, I am such a silly man,
Please find some pity in your heart, just a little if you can,
I'm cursed with this dribbling everywhere I go,
The only time it ever stops,
Is when I stuff my mouth with dough,
I've tried and tried a life straight 'n' free from crime,
But just when things start going right,
I'm let down by slobber slime."

"For your story Double R, I have pity in my heart,
I think you need a chance to make a brand new start,
I believe I have a job for you stamping all my post,
The butler licks stamps every day,
His tongue's as dry as toast."

Double R took the job of the Royal Stamp Licker,
Letters to foreign kings and queens,
No one licked 'em quicker.

At work on his hundredth birthday,
He sank back in his chair,
When his last letter to lick,
Caught him in a stare.

Dear Sir Roderick Robinson,
The Royal Stamp Licker,
No one in the Palace has ever stamped them quicker,
So I'm making you a Sir, on this very special day,
Thanking you for years of service,
And your loyalty all the way.

He climbed up into bed that night,
The happiest he'd ever been,
Aching and exhausted,
He slipped into a dream,
Blissfully unaware,
He'd licked his last stamp for his Queen.

THE END

LET'S TALK ABOUT THIS STORY

1. What jobs did Roderick Robinson try?

2. What was the name of the Inspector?

3. What was Roderick's disguise when he broke into Buckingham Palace?

4. How many laser beams did Roderick count surrounding the Queen's crown?

5. What did Roderick Robinson wrap the Queen's crown in?

6. What was the job the Queen gave to Roderick Robinson?

7. Do you like Roderick Robinson even though he was a robber?

CAN YOU SPOT 10 DIFFERENCES BETWEEN THESE 2 PICTURES?

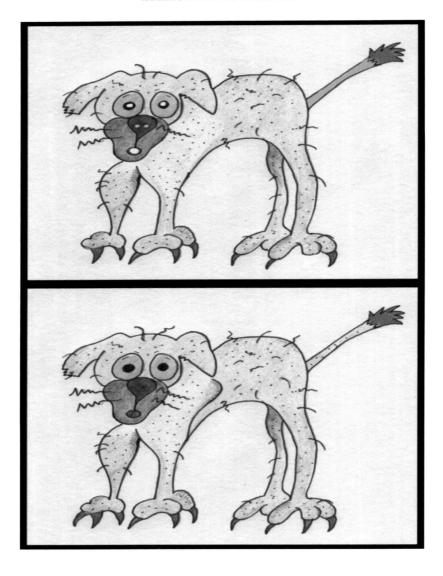

CAN YOU COMPLETE THESE RHYMING COUPLETS FROM COPS AND SLOBBERS ?

1. He bent, split and twisted, tearing his pants at the seams,
   Manoeuvring himself in and out of alarmed laser ?

2. But no one asked for Roderick's slobber in their food,
   It really was enough to make you ill, and spoil your ?

3. "I'm absolutely frozen and now you steal my crown,
   It looks like your slobbering has really let you ?"

4. "I visited you at home Double R, to find that you were out,
   You left your back door open so I took a nose ?"

5. "There in his arms he steals M'lady's crown,
   Wrapped in M'lady's own dressing ?"

ALL THEY WEAR IS UNDERWEAR

In a town just north of South Delaware,
The folk walk around in just underwear,
It's always been like this since the beginning of time,
They think nothing of it, they think it's just fine.

"Good morning Mrs Vickers!" shouts Mr Joe Gants,
Marching along in just underpants,
"Good morning Joe," replies Mrs Pam Vickers,
Strolling along in her bra and her knickers.

In the queue at the bank stands Chief O'Rundies,
Wearing a brand new pair of blue undies,
Behind him stands Mrs Marjorie Laws,
Flashing her famous pink frilly drawers.

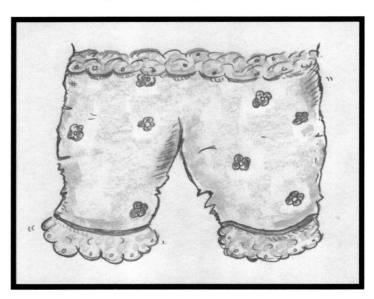

Behind the bank counter working so hard,
Is the stern and the serious Mr Gerrard,
He is famous in town for his outbursts and rants,
And will only be seen in the finest grey pants.

By now I hope I have set the scene,
I trust you're not finding it overly obscene,
But these people living north of South Delaware,
Were happy and contented in just underwear.

Some say things never stay the same,
And this can be a sad and great shame,
For these folk living happily in just underwear,
Life was uprooted by a travelling fun fair.

The Cordona Fair was famous worldwide,
Their star attraction, a nine hundred foot slide,
They'd visited every nook and cranny of the Earth,
Performing from London to Delhi to Perth.

As the circus performers stepped down off the bus,
Some nearly fainted from shock and disgust,
Waiting to greet them was Mayor Reggie Bo-Hants,
Dressed only in socks and shiny gold pants.

Mayor Reggie Bo-Hants had a very large belly,
And as he shook hands it wobbled like jelly,
The wobbling rippled right up to his chins,
Then rippled right down, as low as his shins.

Last off the bus, was the big boss Ring Master,
Alfredo Cordona De Marco Pilaster,
He stood there frozen in shock and surprise,
The Mayor in gold pants, a sight for sore eyes.

The Mayor gave Alfredo a large welcome embrace,
Then kissed both the cheeks on Alfredo's red face,

About to stop breathing, the Mayor let him go,
Then embraced him another five times in a row!

"So happy to have you, do feel at home,
In trousers or undies, please stroll and please roam!"

Alfredo replied "Is what I see true?
Displaying your undies is simply taboo,
Mayor Reggie Bo-Hants I strongly protest,
Please put on some shoes and at least a string vest!"

Mayor Reggie Bo-Hants laughed out loud,
"Alfredo Ring Master why be so proud?
In our town just north of South Delaware,
We are happy and contented in just underwear."

Alfredo marched off with a huff of disgust,
"We will perform in this town if we must, if we must!
Ring Master Alfredo will think up a plan,
One way or another, there'll be an underwear ban."

Now Alfredo knew people in very high places,
Among certain circles, he was one of the faces,
The first thing he did was bring in the press,
First on the scene, the Evening Express.

The Evening Express sent Maxfield McSnorter,
Famous for being a low life reporter,
His story was all, the facts never mattered,
Many a life McSnorter had shattered.

His side kick and partner, who caught it on film,
Was the crafty and devious Miss Monica Milm,
She was lacking in morals, she showed no shame,
Life to her was one big game.

Milm and McSnorter followed the Mayor,
Snapping him of course, in just underwear,
They sneaked around town and hid up a tree,
The low lifes even snapped him going in for a wee.

Next they harassed him, inquiry and question,
Showing no respect, no tact, no discretion,
"Mayor Reggie Bo-Hants what's wrong with your town?
You're simply not normal, they should shut this place
down!"
The Mayor responded in a sad and glum voice,
"Our town is founded on freedom and choice,
This town just north of South Delaware,
Is happy and contented in just underwear."

Milm and McSnorter sent back their story,
They made it sensational, shocking and gory,
"Read all about it! News that will shock!
Mayor rules town in his pants and his socks!"

Now the Evening Express was a very big paper,
Its influence strong, a public opinion shaper,
Across the internet the story spread wide,
Gossiping about it from LA to Kilbride.

But for the folk living north of South Delaware,
Life was now unhappy in just underwear,
Strangers arrived in buses and coaches,
Swarming the town like a plague of cockroaches.

They pointed and stared, happy to laugh,
In cafés and shops they mocked local staff,
All of a sudden there was nowhere to go,
The underwear people felt bare and on show.

The Mayor held a meeting at the local town hall,
Only locals allowed, no outsiders at all!
"What shall we do? I have no idea!"
"The answer is clothes!" boomed a voice from the rear.

Disguised in just pants, sat Alfredo Ring Master,
"I've opened a shop, it will avoid you disaster!
I've got clothes galore at very low prices,
Dresses and suits in everyone's sizes!"

The Mayor cried out "Think what you're doing!
Don't spoil this town, don't bring it to ruin,
We've lived like this since the beginning of time,
We think nothing of it, we know it's just fine!"

Finished speaking he glanced around the hall,
It was totally empty, not a soul left at all,
Doors slamming shut as the last person went,
Now in the shop, big money being spent.

Within a few hours, all the folk fully clothed,
The shop was sold out, lights off and now closed,
Look through the window Alfredo was seen,
Counting his money, such a mean, ugly scene.

Alfredo now done, the Fair upped and it went,
They packed up their tents, no time to repent,
In this town just north of South of Delaware,
No one was seen in just underwear.

All of a sudden big clothes stores moved in,
The pressure was on to look fashionable and thin,
Piles of washing they now had to do,
Mountains of ironing to wade their way through.

A happy go lucky, fun and free place,
Had the smile and twinkle wiped clean off its face,
The underwear gone with their ignorant bliss,
Replaced by new worries "Is my bum big in this?"

But Mayor Reggie Bo-Hants was devising a plan,
"I'll save my town with a humongous fan,
Our last resort, all my hopes are now pinned,
On creating one heck of a gale force wind."

So he set to work, beavering away,
Working all night and working all day,
His gigantic fan was as big as a bus,
With steering wheel and wheels,
It moved with no fuss.

The Mayor called together all the town's people,
"Meet in the town square, beneath the town's steeple,
It's vital you turn up next Saturday,
I have something to show you, to blow you away!"

Before the big day he worked the night through,
Painting the town square in slow drying glue,
The people arrived on time and as planned,
The square now buzzing and totally jammed.

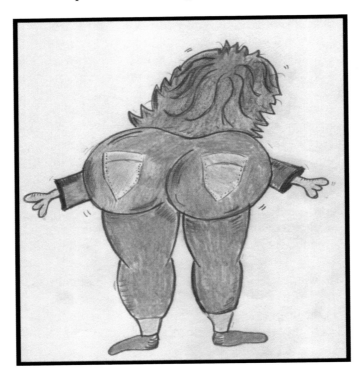

Up pulled the Mayor in his gigantic fan,
The glue should be dry, time to action his plan,
As the folk now realised they were glued to the ground,
The fan started whirling around and around.

Slowly but surely, quicker and faster,
Would the fan work or be an utter disaster?
Now at full speed, a wind of great force,
First thing to fly was the wig on Jack Morse.

Next to blow off was the hat on Miss Toff,
Stuck to the ground, folk's clothes ripping off,
Everything was going according to plan,
He just had to time turning off his great fan.

Trousers tore off, dresses and tops,
Left only in underwear. their shoes and their socks,
When the last pair of jeans ripped off big Bill McCann,
Mayor Reggie Bo-Hants switched off his great fan.

Shocked and in silence, hair stuck in the air,
All now aware of this scene in the square,
Once again just north of South Delaware,
The folk were all dressed in just underwear.

"Good morning Mrs Vickers," spoke Mr Joe Gants,
Standing again in just underpants,
"Morning Joe," replied Mrs Pam Vickers,
Stood once again in her bra and her knickers.

Right in the middle stood Chief O'Rundies,
Wearing a pair of his brand new blue undies,
Behind him stood Mrs Marjorie Laws,
Once again flashing her pink frilly drawers.

And as if by the magic of just underwear,
Looking at each other, these words they did share,
"In our town just north of South Delaware,
We are so happy and contented in just underwear."

THE END

LET'S TALK ABOUT THIS STORY

1. What was the colour of Chief O'Rundies underpants?

2. Name three places where the Cordona Fair had visited?

3. What is the name of the Ring Master?

4. Where did the reporters hide to take photos?

5. On which day did the Mayor call a meeting in the town square?

6. Who was the last person to have their jeans ripped off by the fan?

7. Do you think there is a message for us all in this story?
If so, what is that message?

CAN YOU SPOT 5 DIFFERENCES BETWEEN THESE 2 PICTURES?

CAN YOU COMPLETE THESE RHYMING COUPLETS FROM THE STORY?

1. Behind him stands Mrs Marjorie Laws,
   Flashing her famous pink frilly ?

2. Some say things never stay the same,
   And this can be a sad and great ?

3. He stood there frozen in shock and surprise,
   The Mayor in gold pants, a sight for sore ?

4. Up pulled the Mayor in his gigantic fan,
   The glue should be dry, time to action his ?

5. Shocked and in silence, hair stuck in the air,
   All now aware of this scene in the ?

6. In our town just north of South Delaware,
   We are so happy and contented in just ?

GOING ON A BAT HUNT

Tonight's the night, I'm sure of that,
Tonight's the night, I'll catch the bat,
Tonight's the night, I won't get frightened,
Even when my nerves are heightened.

I'll take my net and I'll take my torch,
I'll take my stick from my front porch,
I'll pack a drink and I'll pack a sandwich,
I'll practice speaking in bat language.

I'm now outside, it's dark as night,
I think I'll call on my friend Mike,
I think I'll be less scared as two,
Ding dong, Mike's in and coming, "Phew!"

Down the street we turn and head,
The bats are in allotment sheds,
Up the lane we quietly trot,
Must not tread on Knoxy's plot.

The story goes that Mr Knox,
Is worse than having chicken pox,
If you're caught on Knoxy's plot,
They say that that's your final lot.

There was a boy called Stevie Reams,
Who once stole Knoxy's runner beans,
The story goes that Mr Knox,
Chopped Stevie up into compost.

Mike points and says, "Look over there!"
I turn and look and now I stare,
It's Knoxy's shed, old grumpy knickers,
In the window a candle flickers.

"Let's go and look" I hear Mike say,
I say, "Perhaps in the light of day"
But Mike's already on his way,
I fear we'll end up Knoxy's prey.

Down in the dirt on all fours,
Crawling, creeping on our paws,
Closer, closer, nearly there,
To the sky I say a prayer.

In the glass a face appears,
It's old and bearded with big ears,
We leap four feet high in the air,
This shadowy face causing such a scare,
We fall splat back into the mud,
I bang my head with an almighty thud.

"What you boys doing 'ere!?"
Knoxy says with a dreadful sneer,
I mutter a reply in voice so slight,
"We're trying to catch a bat tonight."

Knoxy looks straight down at us,
"Are you two boys whom I can trust?"
"Yes Mr Knox, yes you can,
His name's Mike and my name's Stan."

Old Knoxy beckons us into his shed,
My stomach filled with fear and dread,
Then before us such a magical sight,
It filled my heart with warm delight.

Old Knoxy's shed was full of cats,
Foxes, squirrels, mice and bats,
A pigeon wrapped up in a sweater,
"Blimey O' Riley he's making them better!"

We stayed and helped for what seemed hours,
Feeding berries, nuts and flowers,
We promised Knoxy we'd never tell,
Then we bid him a fond farewell.

Now every year about the same time,
Mike and I slip out at nine,
To the allotments we quietly head,
To help old Knoxy in his shed.

THE END

CAN YOU SPOT 5 DIFFERENCES BETWEEN THESE 2 PICTURES?

CAN YOU COMPLETE THESE RHYMING COUPLETS FROM GOING ON A BAT HUNT?

1. I think I'll be less scared as two,
Ding dong, Mike's in and coming ?

2. The story goes that Mr Knox,
Is worse than having chicken ?

3. Down in the dirt on all fours,
Crawling, creeping on our ?

4. Knoxy looks straight down at us,
"Are you two boys whom I can ?"

5. Old Knoxy's shed was full of cats,
Foxes, squirrels, mice and ?

ABOUT THE AUTHOR

Jason Hall is an established writer and illustrator of children's rhyming stories and poetry. It first started with a poem for his daughter called "The Magic Watering Can".

He has performed many readings and poetry workshops in schools and libraries across London and Surrey. His rhyming stories are descriptive, imaginative, thrilling and funny - having audiences captivated from start to finish.

Jason is married with 3 children and lives in Surbiton, Surrey.

For news about new releases please see:

www.jasonhallstories.co.uk

www.facebook.com/jhallstories